Once upon
a time ...

To Charlotte, with love
T.K.

For Helena, the most adventurous princess I know
J.L.

First published 2022 by Walker Books Ltd
87 Vauxhall Walk, London SE11 5HJ

10 9 8 7 6 5 4 3 2 1

Text © 2022 by Timothy Knapman
Illustrations © 2022 by Jenny Løvlie

The right of Timothy Knapman and Jenny Løvlie to be identified
as the author and illustrator respectively of this work has been asserted
in accordance with the Copyright, Designs and Patents Act 1988

This book has been typeset in Mrs Eaves

Printed in China

British Library Cataloguing in Publication Data: a catalogue record
for this book is available from the British Library

ISBN 978-1-4063-8760-5 (hbk) • ISBN 978-1-5295-0787-4 (pbk)

www.walker.co.uk

WALKER BOOKS
AND SUBSIDIARIES
LONDON · BOSTON · SYDNEY · AUCKLAND

PRINCESSES
BREAK FREE

Timothy Knapman

illustrated by Jenny Løvlie

Once upon a time ...
there were lots of princesses
who all did what princesses
were supposed to.

When they were carried off
by a fire-breathing dragon ...

given a poisoned apple
by an evil queen ...

or stuck in a tall tower
by a wicked witch ...

they waited.

Until, eventually,
handsome princes
came along and rescued them.
And they all lived happily ever after.
That was their story.

The End

"But that's BORING!"
said Princess Tilly.

She had a different story to tell.

"I can't spend my life waiting to be rescued!"

So the very next day, when Tilly
was captured by a dragon,

she just rescued herself ...

with a parachute ...

made from knickers!

"Stop right there!" said her Fairy Godmother.

"Princesses don't rescue themselves!

And certainly not with a parachute made from knickers!"

She immediately put Tilly in Princess Prison.

"That's not fair!" cried Tilly.

"You'll stay here until you have learned
to do what princesses are supposed to!"
sighed her Fairy Godmother.

In Princess Prison, Tilly was supposed
to learn how important it was for a princess to sit prettily
and wait to be rescued by a handsome prince ...
and wait ...

and wait.

But that was ...

"BORING!"

And Princess Tilly had
a different story to tell.

"This puny prison can't hold me!"
So Tilly did what she did best —
she rescued herself!

"Hey!" gasped a princess who was waiting to be rescued from a tall tower. "I didn't know you could do that."

"You can do anything you want," Tilly called up to her.

"Can I?" said the princess.

So they hopped onto a couple of passing
swans and flapped off to freedom.

Soon, new stories were spreading all across the kingdom.
Stories of princesses who were scaling mountains,
exploring jungles, and sailing the seven seas.

For the first time, princesses everywhere
were doing exactly what they'd always
WANTED TO!

It was wonderful.

But now the witches, dragons and evil queens
had no princesses to pick on and nothing to do.

The witches had always wondered what it
was like to be stuck in their own tall towers.
So they decided to give it a try.

It was a change.
It was strange.
It was

FUN!

It was so much fun that the dragons tried being
carried off to see if they'd like it.

The evil queens made great big
mushy pies out of all their apples and ...

SPLAT!

They had a great big mushy apple pie fight.

"Can we join in?" asked the princes.

"We can ALL do anything we want!"
cried the princesses.
"We can BE whoever we want!" sang Tilly.
Some of the princes realized
that they actually liked being rescued.

It made a nice change.

So from then on, everyone
took it in turns to try something new;
the princesses, the princes, the witches,
the dragons, the evil queens ...

even the Fairy Godmother had a go!
Until, at last, everyone was doing exactly what
they'd always wanted to.

And this time, they all
really did live happily ever after.